Designed by Bill Foster of Albarella & Associates, Inc.

Distributed to schools and libraries
in Canada by
SAUNDERS BOOK CO.
Collingwood, Ontario, Canada L9Y 3Z7
(800) 461-9120

Library of Congress Cataloging-in-Publication Data
Bunting, Eve, 1928-
The space people/Eve Bunting.
p.   cm. – (Science fiction)
Summary: Two young sisters have an unusual adventure
when they are picked up by a space ship.
ISBN 0-89565-765-1
[1. Science fiction.]   I. Title.   II. Series: Science fiction
(Mankato, Minn.)
[PZ7.B91527So   1991]
[Fic]—dc20
                                    91-16360
                                      CIP
                                      AC

THE
SPACE PEC

THE SPACE PEOPLE

Eve Bunting

Illustrated by

Duane Krych

T H E   C H I L D ' S   W O R L D

*C*asey wakened and heard her fox barking.

The light was early morning grey, the kind that comes before sunup. She lay, listening. There it was again…a high, short snapping bark with something of fear in it.

Casey got quietly out of bed, making sure that the covers stayed over her little sister, Tuck, Tuck lay on her stomach. Flopsy, her old raggedy cloth rabbit, poked out from under her. Tuck and her dumb rabbit!

Casey tip-toed along the hallway and through the kitchen. The screen door at the back squeaked as she eased it open.

Outside the grass was damp under her bare feet. She pulled her nightgown as high as her knees and ran behind the woodshed where the pen was.

Fox stood huddled in one corner. Once the pen had held a badger and once a raccoon.

Fox's muzzle pointed toward her. His eyes glowed green and wild.

"What's the matter, Fox? Casey crooned. "You're all right. I'll bring…"

"Casey?" There was a tug at her

nightgown, and Casey swung around.

"Oh my gosh, Tuck! You scared me half to death!"

Tuck stared up at her. Flopsy hung all wet and draggly from her hand.

"I woke up, and you weren't there," Tuck said.

"You dumbo," Casey said. "Now you're all cold. Run on back. I'll be in in a sec. And didn't I tell you not to bring Flopsy down here. Fox *eats* rabbits!"

"Oh, oh." Tuck put Flopsy behind her back. "When are you going to let Fox go, Case?"

"When I'm ready," Casey said sharply. "And I wish you and Mom and Dad would quit bugging me…" She stopped, staring up at the sky.

"What's that?"

A round ball of light hung against the grey of the morning. It was so bright that it hurt to look at it. "It must be a meteor or…"

A strange sound came from Fox. It was a whimpering, almost a whine. His red fur was ruffled and spiky.

"It's coming down," Tuck said, "It's funny looking."

"Let's go and waken Dad." Casey grabbed Tuck's hand. There was a noise coming from the light, a high whistling, like a kettle blowing steam. Now the ball of light was between them and home. It was low, hanging just a few feet above the meadow, so dazzling that it was suddenly impossible to look at it.

"In the woodshed!" Casey said. Her hand felt behind them for the door latch. Suddenly a white beam came from the dazzling light ball. It was a finger pointing toward them. Casey's body stiffened. She tried to move, but she couldn't. She tried to speak, but her mouth was numb. Even her brain seemed frozen, unable to believe what she saw.

The searchlight stayed on them, but the brilliance of the ball flickered and dimmed. It was a spacecraft like a silver frisbee, twice as big as their feed barn. Lighted windows circled it, and the beam came from the top. The craft hung motionless. Then three metal legs came out from underneath and fixed the ship to the ground. A part of its curved side slid up and disappeared, and there was an opening. A ladder, a moving ladder like an escalator, uncoiled from inside. The high, soft whine still came from the machine; but everything else seemed filled with a strange, waiting silence.

Someone, something was coming down the escalator.

"If we could get out of the light...out of the light...out of the light..." Casey thought. But the light held them, and there was no way to move.

Two someones came down the steps...three, four. The curved door rolled closed behind them.

They were little, no bigger than Casey; and they were silver, like their craft. On their heads were big glass bubbles, and they walked jerkily on stiff legs.

Casey watched them coming closer and closer. "If we could get out of the light," she thought. Panic choked her, made her want to whimper. Who were they? What did they want?

As they passed through the light's beam, they were suddenly transparent. She could see the bones beneath the silver skin. Skeletons…walking skeletons!

The light went off.

Casey reached for Tuck in the sudden dazzle of darkness. Her voice was back.

"Run, Tuck! Run!"

But hands were on her arms…silver hands. She heard Tuck sob.

Casey was being lifted off the ground. There was one of the silver people on each side of her, and they carried her easily as though she weighed nothing.

"Let me go! Let go of me!" She kicked out and found only air.

"Casey?" Tuck's frightened little voice was right behind her.

Casey took a deep breath. "Dad!" she yelled. "Mom! Somebody, help!"

But Dad and Mom must still be sleeping in the big bedroom down the hall, and there was nobody else.

The moving stairs purred them upward. The curved door rolled open and closed behind them.

There was suddenly no way to breathe. A drum seemed to throb in

13

Casey's ears, and she couldn't see. Everything floated in a red mist, but she knew that she was being carried, carried quickly. Something was opening, and she was pushed through. Tuck almost fell against her. Now, now she could breathe. She sucked in the air. The fog lifted from her eyes; the drums stopped beating.

"Casey?" Tuck clung to the skirt of Casey's nightgown. "I couldn't breathe...Oh, Casey, it was awful." Flopsy still dangled from her hand.

Casey stroked her sister's hair. "It's all right. Don't be frightened."

She looked around.

They were in a big, circular room. Windows were all around — small windows, like portholes. There were people, too. Lots of silver people in black swivel chairs by the windows. These weren't wearing the bubbles on their head. The faces were all turned toward Casey and Tuck.

The faces! Casey felt her knees give way, and she let herself sit on the thick, furry, green rug that covered the floor.

The faces! The eyes were round in front, slanting half way around the heads. The mouths were lipless and set so low that there was no chin, just a sharp, jutting point of bone.

Tuck held Flopsy in front of her eyes and began to cry loudly.

"Sh, sweetie, sh!" Casey said automatically.

*S*he didn't want to look any more either, but she had to. The people weren't silver. They wore body suits. The skin on their faces was whiter than any skin Casey had ever seen. She made herself examine the spaceship, searching for anything that would give hope of escape. She and Tuck were in the middle of the room in a glass booth. The glass walls stretched

16

all the way to the roof. Set high in the ceiling were metal discs, like shower heads. There were other booths, too, lots of them, all made of glass so that she could see through the one next to theirs and the one next to that, too. There was a dog in the closest one. It was a German Shepherd. Beyond that booth was filled with piles of strange things. She saw mounds of carrots, the soil still clinging to their roots. There were bunches of wild flowers already wilting, there were rocks, and in the middle of if all stood an old dirty wheelbarrow.

The booths were arranged in squares, like tic-tac-toe. There was a snake in one. It was a little green garter snake, half hidden in the fur of the rug. One held a statue of a concrete horse. It was chipped, and half its tail was missing. Two of the booths were empty.

"I want to go home," Tuck sobbed. "Ask them if we can go home now, Casey."

Casey rapped her knuckles against the glass wall. "Hey," she yelled. "Let us out. You creeps can't lock us up like this."

The white faces watched her with interest. The only response came from the German Shepherd. He threw himself against the wall and growled and barked.

It was as if his bark was a signal.

Casey thought she'd gone mad, or else they'd all gone mad. The silver people began to bark, too, growling and yapping so that the sounds bounced off the glass and echoed against the high ceiling.

Tuck cried even louder, and Casey covered her ears. The sound died a little, and the barking became less. It was almost a hum now, like conversation. Suddenly Casey understood. They were *talking*. The barks were their voices. One silver person clapped his silver hands and came close to their booth. He barked over his shoulder, and a second space person joined him. They peered in at Casey and Tuck. One pressed his face against the glass so his nose flattened. His big eyes were fluid black, and they shone and wobbled like a half-melted jello mold.

Tuck shrieked, and that made all the people start barking again. Casey thought they might be angry. Or maybe they were laughing. There was no way to tell.

The whistling teakettle sound got louder, and there was a shudder under their feet. High on a platform a silver man pushed buttons on a small red box. The barkers quieted and twisted their chairs toward the windows.

Casey strained to see out. It was too far, but there was a flash of green treetops and then a dazzle of pink streaks against grey. It was morning, and they had lifted off. To where? Oh, to where? They were flying over their house now, maybe over their meadow

where Peter, their pony, grazed. She couldn't bear it.

There was no sense of movement. The whistling had ceased. The silver people looked out of the windows and barked softly among themselves. Sometimes one would come over, stiff-legged, and tap the glass of their booth or pause to stare at the dog or the snake or the concrete horse or the wheelbarrow. Did they know some were alive and some weren't? Did they know anything?

Casey sat with her arm around Tuck. Tuck sobbed gently, and then Casey heard her breathing get deep and steady and knew that she was asleep.

There was no way to judge time, but it seemed perhaps an hour when she heard the whistling start. There was a hurting ache in her ears. They were coming down again. The craft landed smoothly, and two of the silver men put on bubble tops. The door rolled up to let them out and closed again. The others waited. When they came back, they each carried a white duck. The ducks squawked and squirmed, stretching their long feathery necks. The space people barked and snuffled excitedly. The ducks were put in one of the two empty booths. Casey watched how the glass door opened. It was controlled by a button on the floor outside and was so cleverly made that there was no way to tell it had ever been there when it was closed.

Tuck was awake. "Poor ducks," she said sadly, "in a cage. Like us."

The ship took off again. They made another landing, and this time the spacemen brought back a rusty old bicycle and a small gray dog. They put the bicycle with the wheelbarrow and the dog in the booth with the German Shepherd.

All at once Casey understood. Her stomach squelched, and she knew she was going to be sick. But how could she be sick? Where? All these people watching, barking at her. She swallowed it down again. Now she knew. These were space tourists. They were on a trip. When they saw something interesting, they went out and picked it up just the way she and

Tuck brought home shells and things from the beach...Or a starfish, a starfish that had died overnight and begun to stiffen and smell bad. Only now they were the starfish.

When they got to whatever strange planet the silver people had come from, they'd be taken out, played with for a while, and then forgotten. That's what always happened to things you brought back. Then would she and Tuck stiffen and die like the starfish?

"I want my Mommie," Tuck said in a very small voice. She rocked Flopsy in her arms and her tears fell on his bald fur.

I want her too, Casey thought. I want her more than anything in the whole world. She thought of her parents waking up. Her mom would call them for breakfast, and they'd be gone. She still wouldn't worry. She'd think they'd gone outside. She'd think they'd taken Peter for a ride up the Comber trail. Half way through the morning though she'd know something was wrong. Maybe she'd call the police, but what could the police do? They were far away now, far, far away. Would they ever see their mom and dad again? And their house? And Peter?

Casey knew she was going to cry. She couldn't help herself. She let the big hopeless tears roll down her face.

Suddenly there was a tremendous barking. It wasn't the people. There was a different tone to it.

Tuck ran to the glass walls between

the booths. The shepherd and the gray mongrel were locked together in a fierce fight.

Tuck rapped the glass. "Don't! Stop it dogs!"

The big shepherd was at the little gray's throat. Saliva hung in silver threads from his mouth. The mongrel tried to break away, throwing himself against the wall; but the big dog had him again. He tore at an ear. Blood flecked the glass. The people came from their chairs and clustered around. Their yelping mingled with the dogs' growls and groans. The ducks quacked nervously, and above it all was the high whine of the craft preparing for take-off. Then Casey heard something else. The small hiss of the three metal legs coming down again to anchor them to earth.

The shepherd had the mongrel by the neck, and he shook him. The small dog hung, limp and boneless as Flopsy.

Two silver men strode into the booth. They pulled the dogs apart. One of them laid the mongrel in a corner. The German Shepherd faced the second man, teeth bared, a low, killer growl coming from deep in his throat. The silver man swung him up. The dog's jaws closed on the silver wrist, but Casey saw no blood. Was the silver suit so protective then, or didn't the space people bleed? She remembered the skeleton shapes in the light beam. What did the silver suits hide anyway?

The side of the ship rolled up, and the spaceman carried the big dog outside. He came back alone. In a few seconds they took off again.

*T*his time they traveled for a long while without stopping. Casey looked wildly around the circular room. There must be *some* way to get free. But what if they'd already left earth? Still one empty booth, though. There was a chance they'd come down one more time to fill it.

She studied the four glass walls, the silver people, the pilot on his platform, and she was filled with despair. Her eyes saw the mongrel in his booth. He lay, licking his wounds, gazing through the glass at her with a sad, sad expression. "I know, dog," she thought. "I know." Then her heart began to beat faster. The mongrel! Of course.

She leaned against the glass wall, and took Tuck in her lap.

"Tuck," she whispered. " I want you to listen carefully. Now you must do exactly as I tell you. Maybe we can get away. OK?"

Tuck cuddled Flopsy and nodded. As Casey talked her face crumpled, and she began to cry again. Her thumb eased back into her mouth for comfort. When Casey finished, Tuck shook her

head. "I can't, Casey. Please, Casey."

Casey caught her shoulders. "You *have* to Tuck. Don't you dare disobey me. You know Mom says you have to always mind me because I'm bigger. You better, Tuck Benson!"

Tuck gulped. "Ok, Casey."

"I'll tell you when," Casey said. She slumped against the wall. There was still some figuring to do, but it might work. "Oh please," she thought, "please. If I can even get Tuck away."

The spaceship was coming down. The silver people stretched toward the windows. Casey watched one traveler go out and come back with a good-sized magnolia tree. He had uprooted it, and the ball of earth dropped a soil trail behind him. Casey saw and earthworm fall wriggling in pain on the rug. "Can't breathe, can you, worm?" She rapped the glass and pointed to it. One of the silver people picked it up and quickly put it in the booth were the tree was wedged. "All booths filled," Casey thought. "We have to act now, or we're finished."

"Now," she told Tuck. "And you better do it well, or I'll be mad — really, really mad." She stared at Tuck. "Hard as you can, and scream."

Tuck pouted. "But Casey…"

"Do what I tell you." She pinched Tuck hard on her arm. "Come on."

Tuck threw herself on Casey, punching and pummeling; and Casey began to scream.

All the white faces turned toward

them.

Was the whistling getting louder? Were they taking off anyway?

"Harder, Tuck, Harder!" she yelled.

Tuck pulled at Casey's hair. She kicked Casey's legs. She clawed at her face, and Casey felt the heat of blood.

Tuck stopped. "Oh, Casey, I'm sorry."

"Keep going," Casey hissed. "Don't you dare quit."

Tuck closed her eyes and jabbed at Casey's nose. Casey felt the pain, the sickening numbness.

"Good, Tuck," she said thickly. She lay down and protected her head with her arms. Outside was a blur of silver. The white faces and black eyes seemed to move slowly around in widening circles. "Come on," she begged silently. "One of you, come."

The glass door was opening.

"Kick at me, Tuck," she muttered. "Don't stop now." She wet her lips. "Remember, if they…if they let you off. You won't…know where you are. Go to a house. Tell…tell them where you live. We could be in Australia…or anywhere. But they'll get you home."

"Oh, Casey!" Tuck was sobbing. She threw herself on top of her sister, nuzzling her face.

Two silver men came in the booth. One pulled Tuck away. Behind him, Casey saw the curved wall of the spaceship open. It was going to work!

Flopsy lay spread-eagled on the floor, and Casey picked him up. She was dizzy, so dizzy that she couldn't seem to stand. The silver spaceman put his arms under her and raised her. His grip was gentle as if he knew how much she hurt.

And then...and then...Casey saw what was happening. He was going to free *her*. The first spaceman was laying Tuck in the corner the way they'd done with the mongrel dog.

"No!" Casey screamed. "She's too little. Let *her* go!"

But the space people only stared at her.

Tuck crouched in the corner, her eyes glazed, her thumb in her mouth.

"Wait, please wait," Casey begged. "Don't make me go. Let me stay with her."

Now they were outside the booth. A bubble top was fitted on the silver man's head, and Casey was struggling, fighting to breathe. The glass wall closed, and Tuck was inside.

Through the suffocating mist Casey heard the people barking.

Then she was being carried down the escalator. There was sun and sky, and she could breathe.

The silver man set her down. Above them the spaceship loomed. The sound of the whistling was shrill in her ears.

She tried to see his face through the bubble. Was there any way, any way to appeal to him? She still held Flopsy, and she saw the old Rabbit shimmer through the blur of her tears. She

39

smoothed his bare fur and held him against her face. He smelled of peanut butter and lollipops and spilled milk. He smelled of Tuck.

Casey held him out toward the silver figure. "Please," she said. "He's my little sister's. She's going to be so…" Her voice broke on the word "lonely."

"I thought you'd let *her* go. The shepherd was the fighter, and you put him out. You must keep the smallest one. Is that it?" Why was she talking to this non-human, non-person creature?

Through the bubble she saw the gleam of his eyes. Something moved in them…some light, some shadow, some understanding. He turned the rag rabbit round and around in his hands and barked once. Then, stiff-legged he climbed the steps.

Casey crouched in the grass. Now the door would curve closed. The ship would take off. Was this happening? Was Tuck inside there? Now there were no tears left to cry, no feelings left to feel.

*T*hen the spaceman came through the open door, and he was carrying…Tuck! Flopsy was cuddled against her chest. Tuck gasped for air, but the blue began fading from her face before they reached the ground.

The spaceman set her down beside Casey, and Casey put an arm tight about her.

The bubble head nodded. The silver hand listed. Again he climbed the steps.

"Thank you," Casey whispered.

Tuck wrapped both arms around Casey's neck. "I'm sorry I punched you. Does it hurt bad? I was so scared, Case!"

"Me, too." Casey squeezed her hard. "And you were great, Tuck. Terrific!"

They watched the curved door close. The three legs hissed up and disappeared. The lights on the giant frisbee flashed, and it went straight up, like a round, shining rocket. They watched it grow smaller against the blue of the sky.

"I wonder why they let us go."

Casey couldn't believe that this wavery, wobbly voice was hers.

"They were sorry for us, I expect," Tuck said solemnly. "Remember, Casey, how we once caught the two frogs in Comstock pond. Remember, they rubbed their heads together, and we thought it might be a mommy frog and her little girl. Or a husband and his wife. Remember, Casey? We let them go."

Casey nodded. Every bit of her ached. Even nodding hurt. Was that it? Was that why they'd been freed? There were so many things they'd never know for sure. Were the space people bad or good? Or were they like humans, all mixed up? Did they have feelings? Did they know about love?

"It was so awful being caged, wasn't it Flopsy?" Tuck stroked the rabbit's fur.

"Yes," Casey said. She thought about the raccoon and the opossum. She thought of the crabs and the tadpoles and the field mice. She thought about Fox. "First thing when I get home, Fox," she promised. "Very first thing."

"Where are we, Casey?"

"I don't know; but that's a roof way over there, among the trees."

A sudden cold breeze stirred the grass and hummed through the telephone wires above their heads. Casey shivered. That whistling sound! Somewhere a dog barked, and she shivered again. Would things ever really be the same in their lives again?

"Come on, Tuck," she said shakily. She took her sister's hand, and together they started walking.

DATE DUE

MAY 0 2 2006		
FEB 2 7 2007		